Table of Contents:

Dedication

This book is dedicated to Frances Okitor, the love of my Life, Susan Ibekwe and Elsa Hannah Ukokwu who always supported this work and through their Appreciation inspired me to write more. I am Grateful!

Acknowledgement

Love is a beautiful thing, it is mutual, it can soften the hardest of hearts and transform the toughest of characters.

Never Give Up on Love!

RHYTHM AND BLUES

You may be absent at the *A* of my
life

But my desire is to be with you till
the

Z of my life.

From the *B* to the *Y*,

U and *I* will stick together for life..

I will hold unto you, for you are my lifeline,

and all my desire is to make you

mine,

all through my lifetime.

With you na for 120 i go die,

Because as long as you dey

by my side, my blood tonic,

my body and hood no go ever dry.

Come rain come sunshine..

Agile every Morning with the sunrise,

Because you have lighted up my heart

like a fire fly..

Hard to believe it all started with a

Smile..

That Heart melting smile!

A heart melting smile, yet like a deep

Freezer your beauty froze my mind,

beclouded my thoughts and gave me

sleepless nights!

For My heart had been shut,

never again was I going to love,

I Had thought,

because with my love many had toiled,

And my heart hurts so much...

Then out of the blues, u came into view,

my heart played rhythms anew,

To ignore I did choose,

but my heart bleeding from being

beaten

black and blue

had begun to play a new

rhythm and blue..

alas! I had fallen for you.

Eternity, with you I now desire

and yearn.

To be your Adam and you my Eve,

I dream...

But I... I shall make it EVEn,

giving you all my attention

that you wouldn't pay any to the

devil..

And together, forever we will dwell in

the garden of Eden,

no need for redemption for we
shall
overcome every temptation....

It always ends in tears, they say...

But for any Tear, with love

we shall patch,

we will make amends andtogether,

forever we shall dwell,

because to ours, there shall be no

end..

I know you might have been hurt

By men whom you put your trust.

and upon your heart, you have put

a lock!

But i promise to pay for it all,

Even if it means sleeping outside

your door every night waiting to

Pick your lock..

Even if it will only leave me with

Shorts,

I promise to do it all,

No matter the cost,

Just give me a shot!

And I will prove your doubts
wrong.

Anything to make you Happy my

love,

For it is my Call!

Now everyday you run through
my mind,
every space in my heart
you occupied.
You have become all that
mattered

in my life.....

This love gave me assurance wey

better

pass chioma's

cos I'm rest assured u no be fraud

u no be like Tu face amaka..

My love for you na genuine no be wash !

...love unfazed even by my hurts,

no doubts!

E no go rust!

We go oil till dawn.

The only thing deeper than my

TRUST

will be my THRUSTS..

We shall walk down the aisle,

hand in hand, gazing deeply into

each

other's eyes

with joy and desire in our hearts.

Yes I do!

Shall I reply,

and so shall You.

A love with no end cos unlike

Romeo and Juliet, our families

shall Consent..

New every morning!

You will be my honey and I, your moon,

your light in darkness.

Waking up next to you

every morning, The best HONEY MOON..

Love so furious, I will be your vin Diesel

and you my Rodriguez....

Nitro in the tank, our love no go go down..

www.ingramcontent.com/pod-product-compliance
Lightning Source LLC
LaVergne TN
LVHW010513160826
845677LV00012B/2839
* 9 7 9 8 8 4 2 3 2 7 0 2 7 *